This book is dedicated to all the silly children with wild imaginations, especially my two daughters, Leah and Jaime—I love you.

Leah's Mustache Party

by Nadia Mike

illustrated by Charlene Chua

It was Halloween night, and Leah stood in her bedroom looking carefully at her costume. She had decided that she wanted to be a pirate this year. Her mom had bought her a black vest, a sword, a pair of striped pants, and a scary skull hat. It looked perfect.

"Leah, it's almost time to go trick-or-treating!" Leah's mom called to her.

Leah took one last look in the mirror. It seemed like something was missing . . .

"You look great!" Mom cheered. "A very scary pirate!"

"There's something missing," Leah said, very seriously. "I need a mustache. All the pirates in the movies have mustaches."

Leah's mom quickly painted a thin mustache on her chubby little face. "There!" she said. "You're ready to go trick-or-treating!"

Leah looked in the mirror. Her face gleamed with joy, and she cried, "ARRRRR!"

Leah ran from house to house, collecting candy, swinging her sword, and yelling "ARRRRR! I'm a pirate!" to everyone she met.

There were lots of princesses and fairies out trick-or-treating that night, but Leah was the only scary pirate on the street!

6

8

The next day, Leah had to put away her costume and her sword.

She missed being a pirate. She missed saying "ARRRRR!" And, most of all, she missed her silly mustache.

Leah decided that it did not need to be Halloween to have fun and dress up, so she asked her mom to draw a mustache on her face while she played outside.

From that day on, Leah wore a mustache whenever she felt like it.

She wore a mustache when she played dress up with her friends. She wore one when she was watching movies.

Some days before school, Leah would ask her mom, "Could you please draw a mustache on my face for me?"

Leah's mom would always smile and say, "Yes, of course, my Leah."

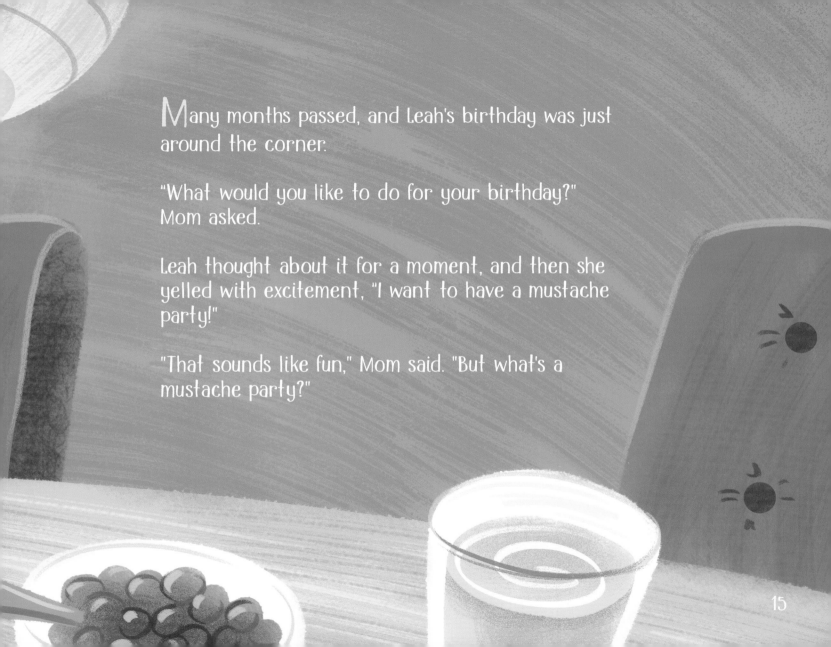

M any months passed, and Leah's birthday was just around the corner.

"What would you like to do for your birthday?" Mom asked.

Leah thought about it for a moment, and then she yelled with excitement, "I want to have a mustache party!"

"That sounds like fun," Mom said. "But what's a mustache party?"

"It's a party where everyone has to wear the biggest, best mustache they can!" Leah replied.

A few days before her big day, Leah and her mom went around town to invite their friends and family.

"Make sure you wear a mustache!" Leah happily told each of them.

18

"Why are you having a mustache party?" one of Leah's friends asked. She had never heard of a mustache party before. Most of her friends had princess or fairy parties with pink dresses and fancy crowns.

"Because I think mustaches are cool!" Leah replied, as she handed her friend a mustache-shaped invitation.

19

The day of the party had finally arrived, and Leah was so excited she could hardly wait to put on her mustache.

"I am going to make my own mustache for the party, okay, Mom?" Leah said. Her mom had made all of her other mustaches, but Leah wanted this mustache to be her very own creation.

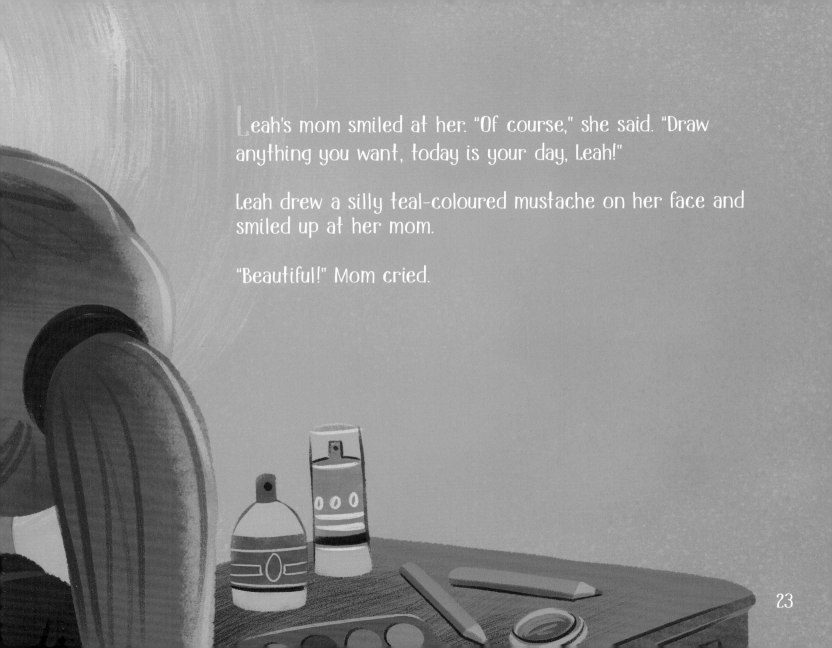

Leah's mom smiled at her. "Of course," she said. "Draw anything you want, today is your day, Leah!"

Leah drew a silly teal-coloured mustache on her face and smiled up at her mom.

"Beautiful!" Mom cried.

When the party finally started, Leah was surrounded by mustaches. There were mustaches on the balloons and a big green mustache on her cake.

Some of the mustaches were big and bushy, and others were short and prickly. Leah's friends even came wearing dresses and mustaches!

At the end of the party, Leah told her mom about all the fun she'd had. "This was the best mustache party ever!" exclaimed Leah. "Thanks, Mom!"

Leah's mustache party had been so perfect that she didn't want to wash away her teal mustache. So she decided to go to sleep with her face still painted.

In bed that night, Leah could not stop thinking about her mustache party.

That was a cool party, Leah thought to herself as she drifted off to sleep.

Mustaches are the best!

· Nadia ·

· Leah ·

Nadia Mike is an Inuit educator, who recently graduated with a bachelor of education from the University of Regina. Although Nadia has lived in many communities across the North, she considers Iqaluit, Nunavut, her home. Nadia has two daughters, Leah and Jaime, who constantly teach her to be less serious and enjoy every day. These two girls have also reminded Nadia of the importance of children's literature, and having stories with settings, characters, and themes that show children that their lives and cultures are important enough to be in books. Nadia loves to travel, cook, sew, and drink strong coffee. In 2014, Nadia published her first book, an Inuktitut-language first-words board book. *Leah's Mustache Party* is her first picture book.

· Charlene ·

Charlene Chua worked as a web designer, senior graphic designer, web producer, and interactive project manager before she decided to pursue illustration as a career. Her work has appeared in *American Illustration*, *Spectrum*, and SILA's *Illustration West*, as well as several art books. She illustrated the children's picture books *Julie Black Belt: The Kung Fu Chronicles* and *Julie Black Belt: The Belt of Fire*. She lives in Toronto.

Published by Inhabit Media Inc. • www.inhabitmedia.com

Inhabit Media Inc. (Iqaluit), P.O. Box 11125, Iqaluit, Nunavut, X0A 1H0 • (Toronto), 191 Eglinton Avenue East, Suite 301, Toronto, Ontario, M4P 1K1

Editors: Louise Flaherty, Neil Christopher
Art Director: Danny Christopher

We acknowledge the support of the Canada Council for the Arts for our publishing program.

We acknowledge the financial support of the Government of Canada through the Department of Canadian Heritage Canada Book Fund.

978-1-77227-081-5

Printed in Canada

Canadian Heritage   Patrimoine canadien   Canadä   Canada Council for the Arts   Conseil des Arts du Canada

INHABIT
MEDIA